What's the Weather Like?

It's Sunny

Celeste Bishop

illustrated by
Maria José Da Luz

PowerKiDS press.

New York

Published in 2017 by The Rosen Publishing Group, Inc.
29 East 21st Street, New York, NY 10010

First Edition

Managing Editor: Nathalie Beullens-Maoui
Editor: Caitie McAneney
Book Design: Michael Flynn
Illustrator: Maria José Da Luz

Cataloging-in-Publication Data

Names: Bishop, Celeste.
Title: It's sunny / Celeste Bishop.
Description: New York : Powerkids Press, 2016. | Series: What's the weather like? | Includes index.
Identifiers: ISBN 9781499423594 (pbk.) | ISBN 9781499423617 (library bound) | ISBN 9781499423600 (6 pack)
Subjects: LCSH: Sunshine–Juvenile literature. | Weather–Juvenile literature. | Sun–Juvenile literature.
Classification: LCC QC911.2 B57 2016 | DDC 551.5'271–dc23

Manufactured in the United States of America

CPSIA Compliance Information: Batch #BS16PK: For Further Information contact Rosen Publishing, New York, New York at 1-800-237-9932

Contents

It's warm and bright outside.
It's sunny!

The sun comes up in the morning.

It's a big circle in the sky.

I play outside when it's sunny.

8

My friends play outside, too!

We like playing soccer.

I score a goal!

The sun makes us hot!

We eat ice cream to cool off.

On really sunny days,
my family goes to the beach.

It helps us cool off.

My mom says too much sun
can hurt my skin.

I wear sunscreen.

I also wear sunglasses in the sun.
They keep my eyes safe.

18

19

The sun helps people and plants.

Plants use the sun to make food.

The sun goes to bed at night.